Cheers!
Chelsea G. Summers

AN UNNAMED PRESS BOOK

Copyright © 2024 by Chelsea G. Summers

All rights reserved, including the right to reproduce this book or portions thereof in any form whatsoever. Permissions inquiries may be directed to info@unnamedpress.com

Published in North America by the Unnamed Press.

www.unnamedpress.com

Unnamed Press, and the colophon, are registered trademarks of Unnamed Media LLC.

Paperback ISBN: 978-1-961884-16-8

This book is a work of fiction. Names, characters, places and incidents are wholly fictional or are used fictitiously. Any resemblance to actual events or persons, living or dead, is entirely coincidental.

Cover design and typeset by Jaya Nicely

Manufactured in the United States of America

Distributed by Publishers Group West

First Edition

An Excellent Host

Chelsea G. Summers

THE UNNAMED PRESS
LOS ANGELES, CA

To Tory and Kathleen, with whom I have shared

many glasses of wine,

and to Taylor Swift, with whom I would like to

An Excellent Host

It is Friday, and we are meeting to worship. Callista is bringing her famous gigantes plaki; ask as often as you like, she'll never reveal the recipe. The most she'll say is that fennel is the secret to cooking beans, but we all know that. Whose refrigerator is without fennel? Only that of a barbarian.

Don't think the wrong thing—there's no fuddy-duddy proselytizing for us. Join us in our religious devotions or not, it's no skin off our leopard-print hides. You wouldn't look at us and think that we're lips-deep in religion. We don't wear our sleeves to cover our elbows or our skirts to cover our knees. We slip our feet into our high heels one stiletto at a time, just like any other woman. But we contain multitudes, and we mean that literally, not merely in a "Song of Myself" metaphorical sense. There's nothing demure about the lipstick we wear, and we tend to favor more or less the same shade of scarlet.

Together, we have felt the singular ecstasy that comes from prayer and from religious sacrifice. It sets us apart. We think it sets us above. For without faith, what is a human? No more than an animal with a FICO score. We believe it's our obligation as sentient beings to give over to God and let Him move through us. In God we trust; for God we must; through God we lust; with God we thrust.

Teeth, check.

Pits, check.

Butt, balls, and back, check, check, and check.

Socks: clean, intact, and matching. Check.

I couldn't find my favorite underwear—the heather-gray hugger-gripper briefs from some Swedish sustainable fashion company, whatever that means. They were an Instagram impulse buy one insomniac night. I decided I'd go commando. Chicks dig commando. It says "bad boy." Commando looks spontaneous, even when you've planned it. Commando, especially under broken-in button-fly jeans, says you're a man who puts his dick forward. You're hot off the block at the pop of your Levi's. You're feral, and you're fearless. Commando says you can take the boy out of Missouri, but you can't take the Missouri out of the boy. It's not called the Show-Me State for nothing.

Almost a decade ago, I moved to New York City from Palmyra, Missouri. I was too much for Palmyra, a charming, dumb, small town just outside of Hannibal, which, sick name aside, is a piss-poor excuse for a city. After living there twenty-something years, Missouri was a snore-fest, but I miss the wild, wide-open blue of its skies. I miss that illogical frontier feeling that lingers in Missouri, despite the reptilian crawl of traffic and big-box stores. I miss the smell of rain blowing through the cornfields that once pressed up against my dad's split-level ranch. The fields don't press so much anymore. Less corn, more suburban sprawl. Too many cul-de-sac couples raising their 2.5 kids, too many even for the moribund Midwest.

Fun fact: Palmyra's claim to fame is Jane Darwell, who won a Best Supporting Actress Oscar in 1940 for her role in *The Grapes of Wrath*. It's not like I'm a huge Jane Darwell fan or anything—she died almost twenty years before I was born. It's that Webster University, located in Missouri's redundantly named Webster Groves, has something called the Jane Darwell Scholarship Award to study acting, and I won it. Without dear, dead, prow-bosomed Jane, I wouldn't have come to New York fuckin' City with a history of binge drinking, a big box of books, a fat cat, a few hundred dollars, and images of my name in hackneyed bright lights on the doubly hackneyed Big White Way. When I consider the brevity of my failed acting career, I think maybe I should've gone west as a young man, but I took a left turn out of Palmyra into Illinois, and I didn't stop going east until I landed face-first in Manhattan. I considered Los Angeles. I visited a few times, went on some auditions, drove around, and saw the sights. Bottom line: L.A. made me feel emptied out, dumb, and sun drunk, a rolling muscled ball of pretty-boy vapidity. Don't get me wrong, I like being pretty; I just don't like feeling it.

Growing up in Palmyra, before I hit the stage at Palmyra High School, I read a lot. Books were my salvation. Mostly modernist works, like everything Hemingway ever wrote. Ditto Faulkner, Fitzgerald, and even Sherwood Anderson. I read Ibsen and Tennessee Williams and Chekhov and O'Neill. I read as a kid, then I acted as a teen. Not to put too fine a point on it, but I was desperate to be anywhere but Missouri, so I was all about living in my brain, whether on the page or on the stage.

Words are why I chose New York City, and the Big Apple hasn't disappointed me, not exactly. It's not what I hoped and it's not what I envisioned and it's not my name, Shad Taggart, in lights or even in black ink in a playbill as an understudy in an off-off-Broadway play, but it's all right. I bummed around the grimy corners of stage acting, and after playing the requisite shady perp in a *Law & Order* lineup and a corpse on *NYPD Blue*, after failing to nab spots in national commercials for car insurance and hemorrhoid relief, and after striking out in one too many NYU student films directed by the next Scorsese, the next Lee, the next Jarmusch, I made a change. I decided that if I was going to sell out, I was going to sell out big. I got my real estate license, and within eighteen months, I became a property owner, moving out of my grungy studio rental in Inwood and into a freshly renovated JR4 with an en suite bathroom in a prewar on the UWS. The co-op board loved me.

It's not my life's greatest passion to sell floor-through apartments to entitled pieces of Wall Street shit, but I can't say I hate the money. And it's not like my acting training is going to waste. I am skilled. I can genuinely pretend to care. I pretend that these people are truly masters of the universe. I pretend that they deserve that Viking range and that recessed lighting and those unobstructed views of the Hudson. I pretend to be invested in their hyperinflated Chanel No. 5— or Invictus-scented visions of themselves, and they believe my honest blue eyes and my thoughtful five o'clock shadow. It's not a bad life, even if my bright-lights, big-city acting dream didn't turned out as I hoped. Or prayed. I was raised Baptist. Whatever. Momma's dead, and Dad never cared about church.

One fantastic thing about New York City is I get laid a lot. Like, *a lot*, a lot.

Not to sound like that half-undressed guy in the Equinox locker room, but I hook up left, right, and center. Thank God for OkCupid, which is a goddamn boundless buffet of fleshy delights in this hard-edged, hungry city. If nothing else, OkCupid has put my headshot to heavy use. God knows that casting agencies never gave a damn about my headshot, so screw it. I might as well find a way for my headshot to benefit me. It's a good picture, even if black and white doesn't revel in the full Technicolor glory of my super-blue eyes. When I was still acting, industry people always told me that my headshot looked like publicity photos of a movie house heartthrob circa 1958. Like I'm the reincarnation of Tab Hunter or Grant Williams or some such nostalgic bullshit. What can I say? My headshot looks exactly like me, even now, a half decade after I sat for it. It's the irony of ironies for an ex-actor, but I can't be other than I am, and what I am, at late thirty-something, is too pretty for stage or screen. Still, my prettiness is a mixed gift: what kept me from being taken seriously by directors brings me a lot of real estate clients, and what kept producers from hiring me makes women drop their misgivings and their panties.

New York City is filthy with people like me—starry-eyed wannabes who have morphed into scaly-souled sellouts—but I remain a rare commodity. And that's because I am a legitimately tall man who is exactly what he seems to be. I seem pleasant, clean, fun, and completely emotionally unavailable. I am these things to my very marrow. I respect the hell out of a woman when I'm fucking her, but as soon as I hear her door go *click* at my back, I am alone in my thoughts.

For tonight's worship, Callista had found him, our delicious treat of a man whom we would entwine in our arms and pull to our lips. It could have happened to any one of us, but Callista has always been lucky. She is the most beautiful, of course. Not that any of us are slouches in the man department—we all have our charms. Georgie is bewitching, Chrysis has the most lustrous gold hair, darkling Philia is incandescently erotic, lithe Naia dances like moonlight glimpsed through swaying fig trees, and rhythmic Myrta, well, Myrta has stamina for nights. There have been others, naturally, and we always want to be more. But tonight we are six. Six women bound by our common devotion and our driving passion and our glasses raised in rapture.

In our congregation, we are only as autonomous as we are connected. Strong, independent women, we gleam as poster girls for the post–*Sex and the City* age, living in the *Sex and the City* metropolis, flourishing in a bustling time of go-girl girlbosses who seem to have it all, if "all" is endless free time, a wardrobe stuffed with Gucci, and no concrete backstory beyond vague gestures at generational or inherited wealth. We go to work at our jobs, doing something; we go to sleep in our apartments, living somewhere; we have "lives," whatever that means. The truth is that we no longer feel connected to our solo, secular selves. In the outside world, we exist in pastel washes of generalities; we grow vivid only when we are with our sister seekers. You wouldn't clock us as different, not at first, probably not even at last. In the year of their Lord 2014, we resemble the many packs of Louboutin-wielding women who prowl clubs, slurp oysters over brunch, and suck down cosmos while dissecting their amours. Cliques like ours abound, ubiquitous on the cobbled streets of the Meatpacking District or in the sleek spires of the Financial District. Groups of fine women stalk Manhattan's chicest landscapes, as if there aren't any lone women left in this city. We six resemble those omnipresent feminine flocks, but we are wholly singular in our interdependence.

Once upon a time, we six found one another, and together we found God. Unique as we are, we're not unlike any woman and her crew of sweetly smelling besties. We're simply much closer. Some of us met somewhere—a wide white sand beach where an uncanny blue sky kisses ultramarine water; a seething concert where women mouth "ever ever ever" as one;

a bar where bloodred wine pours from terra-cotta jugs; a modern dance class where sweat-stained bodies join and split like atoms; a sprawling midsummer picnic party where a drum circle beats, beats, beats like the pulse of a sleeping giant—and we pulled others into the fold. People think we're sisters, though we look nothing alike.

We're tighter with one another than with our blood relatives. We fight with our families, or we did when we still saw them. We never bicker, never scrap. Disputes dissolve like water beading from a glass. Together, we move like a jellyfish, complexly, inextricably connected in life and in death. Our faith is our ballooning bell, the center that unites us, our shared existential meaning that gives each of us purchase in this drifting, turbulent, fathomless world. As human women, we are irrelevantly separate, yet as spiritual congregants, we are united, reverently bound in our euphoric love of our God.

For us, it's the old-time religion—and we mean the *very* old time. Those bearded men in their robes and their sandals are Johnnies-come-lately, ditto that jolly guy with the big, round belly and the bodhi tree. We adhere to doctrine that's almost as old as time itself. Our faith, we like to say, is newer than time but as old as wine.

Tonight's ritual delight is not our first, naturally. There was one who said his name was "Patrick with a 'P'"; he was dumb as a drum but so fetching with that black, black hair and those firm-muscled thighs. The French one, Stefan, who spat out our wine and called for a Bordeaux; he didn't last long. The college professor, Anthony, who was older than our usual selections—his velveteen voice growled from deep in his chest like a beast; we enjoyed him until we couldn't. So many men over such a long time. Callista had procured plenty, but not all, or so Georgie would be quick to observe. Callista is the best at dating—her photographs are breathtaking. In preparation for tonight, she had trysted with tonight's man four times, testing his fitness again and again and again and again before proposing him to us. She liked his scent, she said. It reminded her of pine resin.

"What's his name?" we asked as we formalized our plans.

"Shad," Callista said.

"Shad," Philia echoed. "Like the fish."

"Or the young Hebrew man who survived being thrown into the firepit by that Babylonian king," said Myrta.

"Yes," we whispered, "survived."

"What does he do?" asked Chrysis.

"Everything," answered Callista, and hugged herself in a shiver of remembered pleasure. "But he's a broker."

"He's poor?" Georgie asked, a pout in her voice.

"Not very. But he is tall," Callista said, "just like we like. And handsome."

"Oh," Naia purred, "so handsome."

"Friday, then?" Callista asked, her cardinal-tipped finger poised over her iPhone.

"Friday," we echoed. "We'll book a spot."

AN EXCELLENT HOST

Tonight, I have the most awesome date of all dates. Callista, her name is, and she's bringing her best friend. Possibly best friends, plural. I'm not entirely clear. Like it says on my profile, I'm down for multiples.

Callista, like the TV star. You know, that super-skinny actress from back in the day, head like a lollipop, body like a strawberry Twizzler. Played a quirky lawyer on TV, but married Indiana Jones in real life. I mean, c'mon, Callista—what are the chances? When have you known a Callista? I met my Callista, where else, on OkCupid. We were a 98 percent match, according to the site's survey questions. That was pretty cool. Callista's profile picture showed her tawny face framed by a mad tangle of red curls. The next photo showed her on Fire Island standing topless in a tiny bloodred bikini bottom, some unpictured person's hands holding her globular breasts, the waves and the sun crashing around her. In the third picture, Callista smiled over a big glass of red wine, mouth agape, teeth wild and flashing, lips wine-stained, green eyes winking. Looking at her tiny images on my iPhone, using my thumb and forefinger to massage them into expansion and focus, I was smitten.

Admittedly, I was surprised by her answering yes to the OkC question that asks whether her "religion/God is the most important thing" in her life, but whatever. Callista could say she doesn't believe in dinosaurs, and I'd be fine with it. You know, as long as she believes in birth control.

IRL, Callista delivered everything her profile promised. She radiated, burned. Limbs smelling like flowers and musk. She looked like a fever dream in a snakeskin dress and these ridiculous spike-heeled boots. Drank a bit, but then so did I. We tumbled from bar to hotel bed in a few delirious hours, then we fucked like heroes. Callista came over and over, speaking in tongues, my tongue in her mouth.

Plus, she paid for the bar tab and the hotel room. You gotta love a woman who knows when to slide her platinum AmEx across the counter. Over the next few days, we texted a bit, not too much, flirty phrases peppered with emojis: tacos, lips, peaches, ears of corn, a spurt of water. After that first date, we met up three more times, once every other week or so, always a weeknight. Each time a different part of the city—at the Met Opera House for a performance of *Médée*, at the Brooklyn Museum for a show of Etruscan bronzes, and once for a tasting of Greek wine somewhere in Queens. We watched, we looked, we swallowed, then Callista took me to a hotel, and we had lots and lots of filthy, glorious sex. Sure, I wondered why we hadn't gone to Callista's apartment—most women like to do it on their home turf—but I figured she's like me and needs a separation between the profane and the private. Or she's married. Either way, hotels are awesome.

And she wants to share. It's like I peeled the clothes off a woman and found the golden ticket of twenty-first-century hookups. The only thing I look forward to more than a date where I know I'll get to fuck one lusty lady is a date where I know I'll get to fuck more than one. I'm going in blind, but I like Callista well enough to roll with it. She's hard to pin down. Enigmatic. A woman given to the royal "we," but when you're as blazing beautiful as Callista, I'll grant you all the idiosyncrasies available to man—or woman, in this case. Callista could wear a spangled cape and talk about herself in the third person, and I'd still come running.

So tonight I get to hook up with both Callista and her friend (friends?) at some apartment in the bowels of Bushwick. When I first moved to New York City, a full-on orgy stuffed with clones of Charlize Theron and Naomi Campbell couldn't have tempted me to go to Bushwick, but now, this formerly frightening corner of Brooklyn is more than safe; it's trendy. So many abandoned cast-iron buildings couldn't stay empty forever, not when there are hipsters with trust funds and artisanal breweries popping up like *Amanita* mushrooms after the rain. Not when there are proliferating tech bros and tattoo studios and coffee shops and House of Yes and Airbnb. It was only a matter of time and capital before Bushwick got split open, gutted, refurbished, and repackaged as a destination for major fun. I should look into listings, maybe buy an investment property for myself. Passive income is where it's at.

Chrysis carries her cymbals, clanking faintly as she walks. Philia had opened the wine hours before, and Myrta had unwrapped her tympani, setting them conveniently on a side table. Naia had spent the afternoon bedecking the room in ivy; the greenhouse scent fills our nostrils. As she so often did, Georgie sent a text to say she was running late: it read a clock, a sad face, and a series of women dancing in red. Of course, it wasn't like we weren't aware. The left tentacle always knows what the right tentacle is doing.

"He's coming, isn't he?" Myrta asks as we enter. We hadn't had time to drop our coats.

"Yes, yes, yes. He's coming. He's not the type to renege on his promise," Callista says. She knows him best.

Philia adds, "He's quite excited."

"Wouldn't miss it for the world," we say.

"Be real," Chrysis says, "if you were he, would you?"

We laugh and laugh, and then we laugh some more.

Like those early Christians on the move, hiding out in catacombs, outrunning Roman centurions, our temple is peripatetic. Modern times misunderstand us. As an order, we find ourselves out of joint, our holy worship a source of fear. So it is that we caravan from place to place—but no matter, wherever we go, our God finds us. This Friday night, we convene in this lovely loft on the top floor of a brownstone somewhere in Brooklyn; Airbnb has been a boon to our people. Someone had thoughtfully rolled up the carpets and leaned them against the wall like lazy Doric columns.

"Look at the baby grand!" Georgie says, entering in a mad rush, as usual.

"Yes," we answer, "this place is posh."

"So posh," we second.

Myrta lights the candles and smiles. Chrysis brushes back her long hair and checks her watch. "Fifteen minutes," we murmur.

"Though he's so often late," we say.

"Often late," Callista says, "but always beautiful."

"So beautiful," Philia says. We murmur agreement.

The room looks warm, inviting, gracious, almost as if we lived there. The candles burn like tiny stars, twinkling off the crystal goblets that Naia is arranging on the breakfront. She tweaks a sprig of ivy from its stem and pops it in her mouth. She chews, thoughtful. "Do we like these goblets?" she asks. We assure her we do. "Not too much of a shibboleth?" she asks. We tell her that they are not.

"I miss the gold ones," Georgie says with a sigh. We all sigh. How could we not miss the gold?

Myrta seats herself and pulls a drum to her lap, snuggling a large one between her long, strong thighs. She plays a tattoo over the top. Her fingertips drop like rain, pattering across the hide with fluttering, stuttering staccato. Her palms beat gentle, rhythmic thwacks, as she absently feels for the beat. We sense our hearts lurch and settle, adjusting and falling, rising, and dropping, torquing with the *thump thump thump* into a concert of one. Myrta smiles and lets her hands fall.

"Sorry," she says. "Got carried away."

"So easy to do on a night like this," Chrysis says—or maybe it was Philia.

I swear, Google Maps is the goddamn worst. For some inscrutable, fucked-up reason, it told me to go to the Forest Avenue M station instead of the Myrtle Avenue M station, which meant I had to march miles across Ridgewood to get to the apartment on Beaver Street—yeah, seriously. I was going to Beaver Street in Bushwick to hook up for group sex. Sometimes I love my life.

"Group sex" is an oddly clinical term for an intimate activity. "Group" is a weird word, like "grouper" or "Groupon" or "goop." Say a word enough times and it loses all meaning. Group. Group. Group. Group. Group. Group. Droop. Poop. Excitation often leads to anxiety. Momma raised me to be polite in all situations, which means I feel a strange sense of responsibility for other people's enjoyment. This is fine at your average clothed cocktail party or real estate convocation—I know how to ask people flattering questions and make them feel relaxed, witty, and wise. At naked parties, however, creating this level of comfortability takes more finesse. More finesse, more stress. In a naked party context, making people enjoy themselves means bringing them very specific pleasure. Orgasms, not to put too fine a point on it. And women's bodies are challenging! I've hooked up with enough self-professed feminists to know that talking about women's bodies like unexplored lands or locked boxes or dark mysteries is wrong or bad. Freudian, I've been told. I know that to think of women's bodies in these terms is, somehow, misogynist, but my mind goes there. Women are all so different, and they all want to come, and they all get there in their own highly individual, laser-specific ways. Still, I want them to come. I need them to come. When I do, it's bliss. For me, for them, for us together. The apogee of human experience is shared orgasms. And yet, the fear that this time I'll be outmatched lingers.

I never venture into group sex—man, that phrase sucks ass—without feeling the added pressure that every threesome comes prepackaged with the fear that someone's going to be left out. Odd numbers feel unnatural. You can do more with four. Between my compunction to make everyone feel good and my generalized anxiety about bringing happiness to all the lady parts, I prefer my threesomes or moresomes to be guy-girl-guy, or guy-girl-girl-guy, or guy-guy-girl-guy-guy. Homoeroticism aside, knowing that I'm not the only man in the room with an orgasm commitment makes me less stressed.

I walked, my thoughts spinning out into howling whorls of angst. *Focus up,* I told myself, concentrating on a billowing image of soft female skin. I walked and I imagined Callista's red parted lips and red mop of curls. I imagined her with her friend (friends?). I imagined their mouths on me, my mouth on them, our legs and arms tangled and tight, our skins slickening, a rising funk in our nostrils, candlelight glowing on spit-shiny breasts and butts and labia. I walked and I listened to my pre-fuck playlist: Prince, Rihanna, Ginuwine, NIN, Drake, John Mayer—I know, I'm a cliché.

I walked. In my head, Bushwick called, a promised land of hipster honey and raw milk. I walked faster.

AN EXCELLENT HOST

The door buzzes. Naia, closest to the intercom, presses the button. Without thinking, we arrange ourselves in a crescent line, from Georgie, the shortest, to Myrta, the tallest. As we wait, we count our heartbeats. *Ba-dump ba-dump ba-dump.* We hear footsteps on the floor, *pat pat pat.* There it is, *rap rap rap*, a muffled knock. We draw a breath, exhale, and Georgie opens the door. The hallway light frames him in darkness, tall and man-shaped, just the faintest glint of gold from the light hitting his hair.

"This is Shad," Callista says, and she names us as we stand: Georgie, Chrysis, Philia, Naia, and Myrta. We smile at him, and we say hello, and we let him kiss our cheeks, one after the other, like he is politely sniffing a row of roses.

Shad grins, shining milk-white teeth and Thracian-blue eyes. "You ladies look lovely!"

We smile, and we demur. We love compliments even if we're never sure how to respond.

"Is that wine?" Shad lunges at the breakfront.

"Ah, ah, ah!" Myrta says, arms akimbo.

"We drink together," Georgie explains.

"It's kind of a ritual." Philia laughs and adds, "Let us take your coat."

We slip his jacket down his arms, feeling his biceps, elbows, and forearms as we do. His arms are long, fine boned, but not thin. They hold a manly weight of muscle and a juicy layer of fat. With Callista, we remember his arms. They'd held us, flesh against flesh, skin against skin. We remember his tongue, pink and rough, like a cat's. It had been in our mouths, on our necks, between our thighs. We remember his chest, furred, fluffy and soft. His body is lovely—long and elegant with that nice chest and those manly dips at his hips. From the first, we were enamored of his body. We still are.

The Airbnb flat had been chosen for its cathedral ceiling, open floor plan, and sectional sofa, which rings the living room in an inviting, overstuffed horseshoe. Georgie leads Shad to the center of the sofa and sits him down, toying with his hair, unbuttoning his shirt. We feed him dolmas and dates, pomegranates and praise. We press a tidbit of lamb pastry to his lips. We lick away the crumbs, and we giggle.

"What is this you're wearing?" Shad asks, catching hold of Myrta's wrap.

"Snow leopard," she answers.

He laughs. "It's fake, though, right? I mean, it's not real."

Of course not, we answer. Snow leopards are endangered.

Callista and Chrysis walk around the circle; they place a goblet of wine in each outstretched hand. "Io evohé!" they say, and raise their glasses.

"Io evohé!" we respond.

"Io evohé!" says Shad uncertainly, and then he laughs. "What is that?"

"Just a toast," we murmur.

"A call to God," Georgie squeaks, and slaps her hand over her mouth.

"A cheer to pleasure," we say loudly, and glare at Georgie. She can be so thoughtlessly naughty.

"I'm all for pleasure!" Shad exclaims. "However you say it."

We look in his eyes, we drink, and we drink some more. We run our fingers up his chest and into his shaggy blond hair. We scratch the skin beneath his beard stubble with the ends of our manicured fingernails. We rub his denim-clad legs with our bare calves. We sit on the floor in front of him and press our breasts to his knees.

"You know," says Shad, "this apartment is fantastic. The floor plan is amazing, with those high ceilings. Cast-iron buildings don't usually have this kind of flexibility for, like, renovations. I'd love to know the developer. Do you own or rent? Who lives here—" Shad starts to ask, but we silence his mouth with a kiss.

We pull off his shirt, his shoes. We pop the buttons of his Levi's. We gasp with intentional flattery at the girth and length of his penis. We trail our fingers across his shoulders and down his rib cage. Pushing our shifts off our shoulders, we press our breasts to his mouth, and we press Shad's head to our breasts. We refill glasses and we drink, we kiss and we drink wine out of Shad's mouth, he drinks from ours, and we laugh aloud.

"Io evohé," we say, clinking glasses with drunken disregard. "Io evohé," we say as we finger his fine, pliable flesh.

AN EXCELLENT HOST

When Callista asked me if I wanted to enjoy her with friends, I expected a total of two or three women. I did not imagine a host of six. They were all gorgeous, each so different from one another and all so exquisite. But so many! Six mouths, twelve legs, twelve arms, twelve breasts, six indescribably individual vulvas, twitching and alive and wanting under their dresses. Walking to Beaver Street that Friday night, I knew I'd be outnumbered, but not six to one. Even your reddest blooded American male would feel pangs of performance anxiety in the face of those odds. Taking Viagra had never crossed my mind until the moment I saw those six ladies.

How massive a man do you need to be to rise to the occasion six times? Sitting at the center of those six smiling beautiful women, I realized I was outmatched — hell, I was outmanned. In this scenario, I was thoroughly undone. I was not the banger, I was the bangee. I did the math as one woman after another put some tasty morsel in my mouth, and I concluded that, other than walking out the door, my only option was to ride it out. I'd let them have their way with me, within reason, and I'd lie back and enjoy it.

Already their hands were everywhere, and I let them go where they wanted. Their mouths were everywhere, and I allowed it. They pressed me, pulled me, undressed me, and poured wine down my throat. They bent me and kissed me and licked me and nibbled me with their strangely sharp teeth. I consented at first silently to myself and then I found myself consenting aloud to them. "Yes," I said as they put their fingers in my mouth and my fingers in theirs. "Yes," I said as their heads — red, blonde, black, brown, white-grey, and lavender — dipped over mine, slid down my body, rubbed my skin like big, tawny-coated cats. "Yes," I said as they rolled me over and over, touching my thighs and my knees, my armpits and my nipples, my navel, and my ass. "Yes," I found myself saying again and again, in time to some cryptic tattoo, a dull rhythmic thudding drum that beat in the background. Yes, yes, yes, I said, yes, I want it, yes I want you, yes. Yes, I will drink your wine, yes, I will be your wine. Yes, I want you to swallow me whole.

"Io evohé," Callista/Myra/Naia say as we stream wine down Shad's torso. We pause to admire the wine-dark sheen before running our tongues along his abdomen to catch the drops that pool in his navel.

"Yes," says Shad. He has slipped off the couch and lies puddled on a fur spread across the floor. "Yes," he says, "yes."

Shad's glass is never empty. He sips, sips again, drinks the glass dry, and picks it up to find it full. "Io evohé," we say again and again, and he responds, laughing, naked. His flesh shines in the candlelight, incarnadine. His cock stands hard and free, a branch on the long, limber tree of his body. We toy with it, twirling it with ivy, dripping wine off its tip, licking it up, and laughing.

The air shifts, opens, grows wide with wildness. Is that a breeze? We feel movement on our sleek skins, wet with wine and sweat and spunk. We smell the green tang of moss and the green sharp of ferns and the round umber of dirt. We hear the thwap of a finger on skin, the snap of a foot on sticks.

Beneath our bare feet, the floor feels warm, soft with the dry velvet of old earth. The greenhouse scent of the ivy grows close and hot. Shad stirs, suddenly restive, growing a little frantic. "What is this? Who are you? What are you doing?" His voice aims at urgency, but he slurs slightly. We run our hands down his body, calming him, shushing him. We tell him he's fine. We smile and brush his gold hair back from his eyes, press his taut body back to the ground. We rub our noses on his chin and inhale his smell, tobacco and salt and mint. We feel him relax under our hands.

Philia picks up her flute and presses it to her wine-stained mouth. Myrta's hands skitter over the skins of the drums, *tap-pat-pat tap-tap thump tap-pat pat-tap-tap thump*. Chrysis finds her cymbals and clashes them, *schask! Schask! Schask!* Callista knocks her thyrsus against the floor, *bump-bump-bump*, and Naia claps her hands, twirling.

Chrysis thrusts her arms up and spins, hands high; Philia pulls Shad from the couch, twirling him too, pulling him around and around with us, as we circle and dance like stars in a constellation, wine sloshing out of our ever-full goblets and down our shifts, plastering our silks to our bodies, where we are dressed, and dripping our skin silky and sanguine where we are not. We twirl to the *pat-tap-pat thump* and the *bump-bump* of the thyrsus and the *schask! Schask!* Of the cymbals and the sweet lyric voice of the flute singing over us all. Myrta and Callista, Chrysis and Philia, Georgie and Naia, and all of us together with Shad, the music playing, urging us, moving us, driving us, spinning us around and around. We twirl and we spin, and the room, the city, the sound, and the feel of modernity drop from sight, as if it were no more solid than the shadow of a zoetrope, flickering and faint on the walls. In this temple under the besotted stars, the wind whispers bright and warm on our wet skins, and we dance, our babies forgotten. In the village, our fires burning without us, our voices together calling out to our God, worshipful in fierce ecstasy.

AN EXCELLENT HOST

Do I hear music? Are those stars? What are these women? Panic recedes almost immediately, and I surrender with my internal, eternal yes. I am a trusting animal under their many hands; I am their plaything, their pet. Their fingers stroke me, their nails scratch me, their mouths whisper sounds in my ears, and I feel my body lifted, patted, moved into place. I am theirs, I am nothing, I am theirs, I am nothing. I am theirs.

Everything is as it should be. The damp moss below me, the incalculable stars above me, the sounds of feet pattering and creatures skittering around me, the animal scents in my nose. And the wine, the wine, the coppery, thick, saline wine, I am one with the wine and the wine is good, and these women—these women—they are everywhere, in me, on me, around me, surrounding me, fleshy and warm and wet and hot, and I am theirs. I smell a goat, a lion, another man—or is that a bull? A woman—a new woman, a huge woman, big and broad and looming, smelling like hay and blood and wild animals. I feel the world spin, wrapping me, holding me, carrying me. I am theirs, I am theirs, I am gone in a sob of sweetness.

AN EXCELLENT HOST

We circle and we dance, our hands up high, our voices keening as one, singing and whirling, red in the wine light, and we find the other, the one, the different, the man. We hold him in our hands, the center of our Catherine wheel, and we spin, pulling him, stretching him, wrenching him, our fingers in his flesh, this Shad man. Faster and faster, kiting like raptors we spin, the trance and the ecstasy, the bold and the mad urging us around and around, thicker and faster and more.

His left arm tears first. One arm, then the other. A great fissure down the center of his body, the ribs cracking like a lobster shell, exposing the bright, rhythmic red of his still-beating heart, the tomalley of Shad's tender thymus, the bittersweet mulberry of his liver. He crumples, a paper man folding in upon himself, empty and callow. The legs take more work, but there's little we can't do when we're set to the task. We stop our ceaseless circling; we are steady, intent, bright scarlet in the candlelight, our mouths and chins stained crimson, the hot-wet blood cooling and sticky, iron in our cherry wine, blood thick in our warm earth. Thumping in our hearts, full in our bellies. We press flesh to our lips, and we sing in the sweetness.

We lick our fingers, pulling them deep into our throats, cleaning one another like great, wet cats. We purr in a pile, warm and close; we grow soft again and human, the divine drunk-dreaming in our breasts, our breath quieting to near stillness.

Shad's skin is no longer creamy. His hair no longer glows gold. His eyes no longer shine Thracian blue.

His lips no longer split with a grin—not since Callista ate them.

Poor lamb. He hardly knew what was happening before it was over, before his moment was gone, and he lay in pieces on the floor of some stranger's loft. The end of an ecstasy is always so melancholic. Man cannot live by wine alone, and woman, well, we cannot live by man. Still, we're never alone. Not really. We contain multitudes, we are many, we are maenads, and we will take our pleasures and our revenge. Either way, what bliss.

AN EXCELLENT HOST

Got the Wine for You: A Note from the Author

I am no Swiftie. I lack an encyclopedic knowledge of Taylor Swift's lyrics, and I fail to recognize her myriad gem-encrusted Easter eggs. I didn't follow Taylor Swift on Insta until last year. I balk at dropping a grand on a ticket to the Eras tour, and I'm too cranky to log in to Ticketmaster early enough to score a seat at a reasonable price. To my shame, I don't own a single friendship bracelet.

And yet I wrote this tiny book while listening exclusively to the music of Taylor Swift—and I began writing it in the spring of 2015. What happened is this: in March 2015, a man whom I liked very much ghosted me. I felt enraged, impotent, and bereft, and in a vain attempt to ease my wounded animal soul, I listened to Taylor Swift's albums *1989* and *Red* on infinite repeat. That May, hot on the heels of the ghosting, my friend Katelan Foisy, the same mystic who gave me the tarot card reading that helped midwife my debut novel, *A Certain Hunger*, asked me to be part of Pythia, this witchy event she was hosting in a warehouse somewhere in the bowels of Brooklyn. In keeping with the Delphic theme of the night, and as part of my emotional exorcism, I wrote about a bunch of maenads tearing into a man in an Airbnb in Bushwick. I read the story at Katelan's event. Then I emailed it to the man who had ghosted me with the subject line "In which I kill you." Almost a decade later, I remain amused.

During that frenzied, fucked-up time, writing about maenads hit the right emotional spot—this ecstatic sisterhood exists in both myth and historical reality, a group that meets as much to hard-core party as to exalt the divine. I was drawn to the idea of a feminine collective meeting to indulge in mystic release and misandry. Maenads occupy an interesting space, because while they ostensibly worship Dionysus, the Greek god of wine, they also exist independent of him. As a Dionysian cult, maenads are related to Cybele, a Greek goddess who strides the line somewhere between mother-creator and avenger-destroyer. The loyalty of maenads is, let's say, fungible. Moreover, strung out on grieving this ghost of a man, I felt a bit mad, and madness swirls around maenads. Why else would they convene, drink to excess, dance naked, and tear men apart with their bare hands? Everything about the maenad lifestyle appealed to me.

In my first version of this tiny book—and thank you, American Booksellers Association, for choosing me to write something for Indie Bookstore Day—I exclusively employed the royal "we" of the maenads. I was intrigued by the collective pronoun, no doubt because I felt so alone in my unreasonable, freshly ghosted grief, and I needed to share it, not merely as a work of fiction but as an emotional state. I listened to *1989* and *Red*, and I wrote the story with my heart aching and raw, my demented spirit soothed with murderous thoughts, and my head full of Taylor Swift lyrics. I wanted to get near that ecstatic female rage that suffuses songs like "Blank Space," "We Are Never Ever Getting Back Together," and "I Knew You Were Trouble." The transportive, cathartic, and chaotic energy inherent to these songs felt freeing, even revelatory, so I laved myself in Taylor Swift's delicate, silken fury, and I channeled the maenads' singular consciousness in order to explore this divine and delirious Swiftian spirit.

As I reimagined this story during the winter of 2023—the biggest revision being the inclusion of

Shad's voice—I wrote with the acute awareness of how much had changed in the intervening eight years. It wasn't merely that I had published a book, gotten married, and migrated to Sweden, and it wasn't solely that the world had been changed by a pandemic, the rise of fascism, the widespread banning and burning of books, and the erosion of rights of Black and brown people, migrants, women, and LGBTQIA+ persons. It was also the emergence of Swifties as an economic, political, and cultural force and the massive change that the preeminence of Swifties—or, for that matter, the Beyhive and whatever you call the boygenius fandom—represents to contemporary culture. The world appeared to be waking up to the power of young women's voices. And the old order appeared to shudder at that collective sound.

Way back in the spring of 2015, the term "Swiftie" was still relatively new and in somewhat limited use.

Taylor Swift herself first said the word in a 2012 interview, and she didn't trademark the term until 2017. But by the time I began revising this story in the winter of 2023, "Swiftie" had become more than ubiquitous—it had become revolutionary. If you think I'm being hyperbolic, take a moment to consider the ramifications of Taylor Swift's decision to remove her catalog from Spotify, the importance of her rerecording and rereleasing her early albums, or the $5 billion that Swifties pumped into the economy just in the first five months of the Eras tour.

I rewrote this story as the world witnessed the apotheosis of Taylor Swift, and I re-centered the maenads as a Swiftie-like entity, a group of females whose collective consciousness hung on a shared rapturous experience. I thought about the ways that Swifties embrace the markers of conventional femininity—the will to be pretty, the heightened importance of emotions, the push-me-pull-you negotiation of marking your individual space while in a relationship, the gossamer experience of girlhood—without relinquishing feral power, quiet murderousness, or unshakable solidarity. I reworked this story, and I revisited Taylor Swift's catalog, and I envisioned the glittering, swelling mass behind her. I saw a concert of arms in the air, a shared primal yawp of joy at being in the presence of a modern deity. I tried to dip into that experience, even as I gave voice to Shad (thank you, by the way, to the real Shad, who, ghosting aside, has always been nice as pie).

I was born in the sixties, grew up in the seventies, and came of age in the eighties. I had no Beyhive, no Swifties. I grew into adulthood during a time when young women's voices and experiences were derided at worst or treated as a curious fascination at best. I may be a cast-iron bitch, but I am brought to tears by the increasing, uncompromising primacy of young women's voices. Swifties may be the crest of this tsunami of sensibility, but there's a huge, roiling ocean of young people who feel complex, contradicting emotions and will never, ever shut up about it. They're doing the work of titans, bless them. In insisting upon their importance, in speaking their opinions, in making their beliefs heard, they're changing the world, one Instagram post, one TikTok video, one pop banger at a time. This generation's watchword is "chaotic," and it enwraps conflicting feelings, incompatible desires, and paradoxical impulses in one messy, tumultuous, and elegantly apt term. I wish that as a youth I had allowed myself to be chaotic; I would have felt a lot less pain.

You in the Swiftie generation have changed my life, and not only because you have helped my long-lost disaffected twenty-something find her belated state of grace. Without you, I would not have had the opportunity to write this tiny book. Without the #unhingedwomen girlies, without the #cannibalgirlboss stans, without the people who climb into my DMs to tell me they like my work and call me "mother," my first book would have languished in obscurity. Creators on social media made my debut novel a bestseller, and their collective love has buoyed my sodden, deflated heart more times than I feel comfortable expressing. There are too many social media creators to thank individually, but I'd like to single out Nina Haines, Olivia Koufos, Joseph Hall, Dronme Davis, and David Ruis Fisher, who have undoubtedly annoyed their followers, friends, and family with their passion for my work. I am profoundly grateful for your love.

I'd like to thank my agent, Kent Wolf, who is somehow even more magnificent than his name, and my editor at The Unnamed Press, Chris Heiser, who proposed me to the ABA and worked hard to shepherd this story into shape; I'd likewise like to thank the entire Unnamed staff, as well as my old editor, Olivia

Taylor, who chose to publish *ACH*. I'd like to thank all the indie bookstores who have championed my gory angel baby, and I'd like to shake the hands of the booksellers who suggested my book; I look forward to visiting each and every one of you.

Like Taylor Swift, I am no one without my friends and family. I'm eternally grateful to Tory Jones, Max Fractal, Molly Crabapple, Jen Udden, Sand Avidar, Agri Ismaïl, Jonathan Gray, and Ilana Teitelbaum. You all have my heart. Thank you to the Urdettes, Libby, Anne, and Kathleen, who each dressed as individual Swift eras this past Halloween. Thank you to my dad and my mom for buying me that big illustrated book of Greek myths when I was a kid, and thank you to my aunts, who have expressed endless delight over my first novel. And thank you to my hot Swedish husband, who makes space for me to do my work, sings me goofy songs, and gives me love.

Finally, thank you for buying my stories, for reading them, for talking about them with anyone who will listen, and for telling me you like my book. I wrote it for you. All of you.

PRAISE FOR *A CERTAIN HUNGER*

Shortlisted for the VCU Cabell First Novelist Award

"One of the most uniquely fun and campily gory books in my recent memory... *A Certain Hunger* has the voice of a hard-boiled detective novel, as if metaphor-happy Raymond Chandler handed the reins over to the sexed-up femme fatale and really let her fly."
—The New York Times

"A comic novel, a horror novel, a feminist novel and a moral novel of a kind, *A Certain Hunger* will sate yours—at least for entertainment."
—Los Angeles Times

"A dark, provocative, and wholly incomparable account of sex, food, and other indulgences, marred by just one regret: getting caught."
—BuzzFeed's Best Books of 2020

"*A Certain Hunger* is a swaggering, audacious debut, and a celebration of all the wet, hot pleasures of human contact."
—The New Republic

"*A Certain Hunger* is a macabre banquet of a suspense novel serving up carnal and gustatory surprises... Dorothy speaks like Humbert Humbert and behaves like Hannibal Lecter."
—Washington Post

"Fiendishly entertaining... Summers's shocking and darkly funny novel reads like a feminist-horror version of *American Psycho*."
—***Publishers Weekly,* Starred Review**

"Easy to summarize but difficult to, um, flesh out, *A Certain Hunger*, is, without a doubt, the Great American Female Serial Killer Novel, *The Great Gatsby* of women cannibal foodie satirical black comic memoirs."
—***PopMatters***

"Chelsea G. Summers's *A Certain Hunger* is easily the most distinctive and unforgettable crime novel of this year, a delicious soupçon of satire."
—**Sarah Weinman, author of *The Real Lolita***

"*A Certain Hunger* is as hot and mean and ruthless as its heroine. Summers's novel is a lush banquet of sensory delights, but just under the surface, there's a slick, hard, unassailable core of female rage. This is the monster I didn't know I wanted."
—**Jude Ellison Sady Doyle, author of *Dead Blondes and Bad Mothers: Monstrosity, Patriarchy, and the Fear of Female Power***

"The perfect novel for smart, cultured, angry women everywhere. With wicked wit, *A Certain Hunger* educates, entertains, shocks, and delights, and—if you're not careful—may just tempt you to embrace your inner cannibal."
—**Alma Katsu, author of *The Hunger* and *The Deep***

"This book is crazy. You have to read it."
—*Bon Appétit Magazine*

"Riotously funny and deliriously unhinged, Chelsea G. Summers's *A Certain Hunger* is the perfect send-up of foodie culture, media, and serial killers-as-sex objects. Patrick Bateman and Hannibal Lecter have nothing on Dorothy Daniels, a 51-year-old food critic, who has an appetite for food and life, sure, but also for killing men… an altogether delicious, deranged read."
—*Refinery29*

"Chelsea G. Summers's *A Certain Hunger* reads like a dark, delirious feminist fairy tale. Mordantly funny and lushly baroque, it's *American Psycho* as rewritten by Angela Carter. Irresistible."
—**Megan Abbott, bestselling author of *You Will Know Me* and *Dare Me***

"Unabashedly and full-heartedly living out her id, Dorothy balances her most revolting qualities with a caustic wit, a kind of wink and a nod to readers when things get ghastly that it's all in good fun. After all, she argues, 'Power is the ultimate aphrodisiac.' Move aside, Bret Easton Ellis."
—*Kirkus Reviews*

"You won't soon forget Dorothy or her delicious insights, but fair warning: This book might turn you into a vegetarian, if you aren't already. (Though as Dorothy herself acknowledges, 'It's surprisingly easy to overcome moral qualms, if you give in to the appetite.')"
—*Library Journal,* **Starred Review**

"In this magnetic and satirical debut, Chelsea G. Summers gives us a different kind of food narrative. Dorothy Daniels is a food critic, master cook, and lover of sex. She's passionate about everything she does. Including, unfortunately, murder. This one isn't for the squeamish, as cannibalism is involved, but it is a fairytale-like romp with feminist themes, so if you're looking for a horror-ish yarn that also involves some great food scenes (and not just the human flesh kind), keep an eye out for this one—perfect for those dark winter afternoons."

—*Shondaland*

"*A Certain Hunger* is a hearty novel that, despite its graphic themes of murder, flesh eating, sex, and the dessert menu, is also quite funny. With direct jabs at toxic masculinity and razor-sharp awareness of feminist tropes, Chelsea G. Summers's novel is a slasher-sexy, rich satire."

—*Foreword Reviews*

"Dazzling and gruesome, Chelsea G. Summers has written a gripping tour de force about female friendship, haute cuisine, and how to filet a man and serve him with fine Italian wine. I could not put it down."

—Molly Crabapple, author of *Drawing Blood*

"*A Certain Hunger* is a masterful satire as brilliant as it is deviant. Such a unique work: philosophical, poetic, and all while being funny as hell. Chelsea G. Summers is a damn good writer."

—Mat Johnson, bestselling author of *Loving Day* and *Pym*

"I devoured Chelsea G. Summers's witty, sinister debut in an absolute delirium of pleasure. The murderous recollections of food critic Dorothy Daniels, who only eats the ones she loves, are louche, bawdy, and gorgeously depraved, whether she's teaching us how to mix the perfect cocktail or butcher a human body. By turns filthy and philosophical, Summers' riveting prose tempts us on every page… *A Certain Hunger* stands alone as an unapologetic paean to female desire that begs to be savored with some fava beans and a nice Chianti."

—Amy Gentry, bestselling author of *Good as Gone* and *Last Woman Standing*